Join Daisy and Tom on their Genie Street adventures by visiting them at Ladybird's Genie Street website.

Find out about the latest Genie Street books and meet all your favourite Lampland characters!



www.ladybirdgeniestreet.com

Written by Richard Dungworth
Illustrated by Sarah Horne

A catalogue record for this book is available from the British Library

Published by Ladybird Books Ltd.
A Penguin Company
Penguin Books Ltd., 80 Strand, London, WC2R 0RL
Penguin Books Australia Ltd., Camberwell, Victoria, Australia
Penguin Group (NZ) 67 Apollo Drive, Rosedale,
Auckland 0632, New Zealand

001 – 10 9 8 7 6 5 4 3 2 1


ISBN: 978-1-40931-242-0

Printed in Great Britain by Clays Ltd, St Ives plc

THIS LADYBIRD BOOK BELONGS TO

..............................

Tom and Daisy live on Genie Street, with their mum and dad.

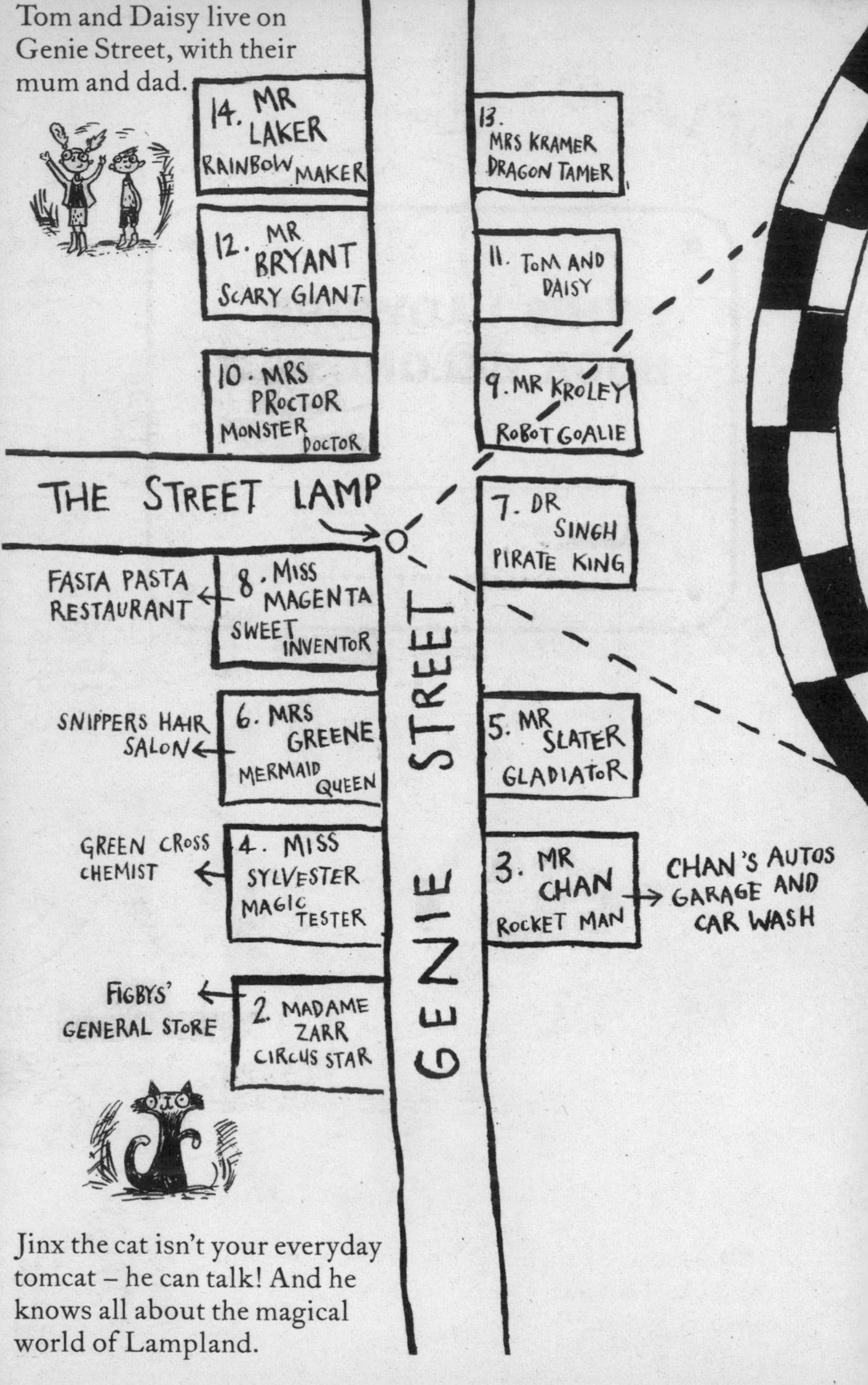


Jinx the cat isn't your everyday tomcat – he can talk! And he knows all about the magical world of Lampland.

# LAMPLAND

Wild Isles
to the Noom
Launch pad
the Seventh Sea
Sweet Factory
Rainbow Meadows
Techno Town
castle Kinghold
City of Ancients
to Crossbone Island
Fairy Forest
Mermaid Reef
Red Dragon Hills
Land of the Giants
Monster Mountains

Mr Mistry, Genie Street's postman, gives Tom and Daisy a special parcel which sends them on each new adventure!

# GENIE STREET

# Dr Singh PIRATE KING

# Contents

# Chapter One
# Missing Jinx

Tom rang the doorbell of number 7 Genie Street. His sister, Daisy, waited on the doorstep beside him.

'Dr Singh is our last hope,' she said. 'Then we've tried everyone on the street. What if *he* hasn't seen Jinx, either?'

Their friend Jinx the cat had gone missing.

Tom tried the bell again. Nobody answered.

'He's probably at work,' said Tom.

Dr Singh worked at the local medical centre – sometimes even at weekends.

'So, what now?' said Daisy.

Tom turned to look across the street. 'Well… there is *one* place we haven't tried.'

Daisy followed her brother's gaze. He was staring at the magic street lamp.

7

'Lampland!' whispered Daisy.

She and Tom knew that the street lamp's magic could transport you to another world. And Jinx knew it, too. He was no ordinary cat. He had shown them the way to Lampland in the first place.

'Maybe *that's* where Jinx has been these last few days,' said Tom. 'Stuck in Lampland!'

There was only one way to find out.

7

The children crossed the road to the magic street lamp.

'Who's going to do the special rub?' asked Daisy.

'We'll both do it,' said Tom. He laid one hand on the lamp post. '*Once up*…' His fingers stroked the smooth metal. '*Once down*…'

Tom took his hand away. Daisy reached for the lamp to finish the job.

'*Then three times round and round*…' she chanted.

7

## Chapter Two

# Half a Bike

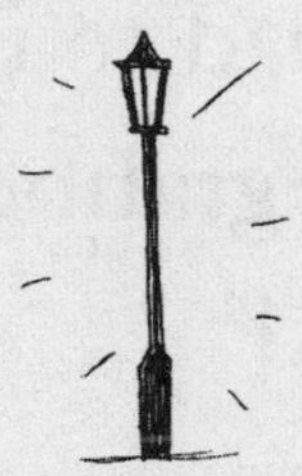

The magic street lamp burst into light. A blazing purple ball shot from the lamp and fizzed through the air. It hit the very door that Tom and Daisy had been standing outside only moments before – the front door of Dr Singh's house. It began to glow faintly purple.

Tom was about to rush back across the road to investigate when Daisy grabbed his arm.

'Watch out!'

Something was coming along the road. It was swerving this way and that. As it zigzagged closer, Daisy saw it was actually *someone*.

'Mr Mistry!'

'Hullo, hullo!' called the Genie Street postman. He was wearing his usual purple uniform and riding a unicycle!

'Whoooaaa!' cried Mr Mistry, as he wobbled up. 'Half a bike is *twice* the fun, bless my ears!' He tossed Daisy a parcel. 'Special Delivery! Whoooaaa!'

The children looked at the address on the parcel.

'That's funny,' said Tom. 'It says *Captain* Singh, instead of Doctor. Look, Mr Mi–'

But Mr Mistry had vanished.

'Come on, Tom!' said Daisy. 'Let's try that doorbell again!'

Daisy never got to press the bell.

As she and Tom hurried back to Dr Singh's front door, it burst open. Bright purple light blazed out of it. They screwed up their eyes against the glare.

The ground lurched. It tipped one way, then the other, like the deck of a ship on rough seas. Tom and Daisy went tottering forward – right into the dazzling doorway.

## Chapter Three

# The Captain

'Shiver me timbers, what's this?' growled an angry voice. '*Stowaway*s!'

Daisy still had her eyes shut. But she knew that she wasn't on Genie Street any more. There was a cool, salty breeze on her face. The ground was still lurching about.

She opened her eyes.

Daisy immediately understood why it felt like she was at sea. She *was*. She and Tom were standing on the rolling deck of an old-fashioned sailing ship.

'*That's* what you arrrrrrre, isn't it, you scurvy dogs? Sneaking stowaways!'

Four gruff sailors were gathered round them, staring. The angry voice belonged to the smallest. He looked rather familiar.

'So, you thought you'd make a fool of Captain Singh, did you?' the man growled. 'Thought you could trick the Terror of the Seventh Sea, eh?'

He turned to his pirate shipmates.

'What do you think, Poggins? Should we throw 'em to the sharks? Or make 'em walk the plank? Or maybe tie 'em to the mast for a while, eh, Pug?'

The angry captain began pacing the deck, muttering about awful punishments. The fourth pirate – a woman with a wooden leg – came closer to Tom and Daisy.

'Take no notice,' she whispered. 'The captain's just in a rotten mood. We've been searching for treasure for weeks now, without any luck. I'm Peg, by the way. Welcome aboard the *Yohoho*!'

Daisy found her voice at last. 'Er... Doctor... I mean Captain Singh, sir,' she began nervously. 'We have something for you. A Special Delivery.'

She held out the parcel.

The Captain glowered at her. He strode over, snatched the parcel and tore off its wrapping.

There was a scroll of parchment inside. Captain Singh unrolled it, still scowling. Then his face lit up.

## Chapter Four
# Crossbone Island

It was a map. But not just *any* map.

'Haa-harrr, me hearties!' whooped Captain Singh. 'This be a map of where Yellowbeard's Treasure lies!' He put an arm round Daisy and gave her a squeeze. 'Thank 'ee, my lovely!'

He seemed in a *much* better mood. He even did a pirate jig.

Tom looked at the map. 'Who's Yellowbeard?' he asked.

Captain Singh blushed. 'Me,' he replied. 'It's a nickname.'

'Yellowbeard?' said Daisy.

'It's a long story,' muttered the captain. 'I had an accident with some custard...'

'But why do you need a map to find your own treasure?' said Tom.

Captain Singh didn't hear. He was already plotting a course for their new destination.

CROSSBONE ISLAND
N
W
E
S
20 Paces
Cove
= YELLOWBEARD'S TREASURE
= HOLLOW TREE

So the *Yohoho* set sail for Crossbone Island – and Tom and Daisy joined the crew.

They helped Peg, Pug and Poggins hoist the mainsail. They polished the cannons. They took turns at the ship's wheel. They even climbed the mast to the crow's nest, to act as lookout.

While Daisy was up there, she spotted something.

'Ship ahoy!' she yelled. 'And it's heading our way!'

# Chapter Five

# The *Black Heart*

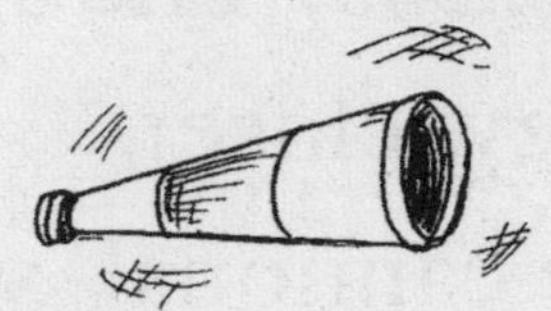

Captain Singh took a long look through his telescope.

'Blasted barnacles!' he cursed. 'It's the *Black Heart*! Captain Corkscrew's ship! He's the most fearsome pirate afloat!'

'I thought you were the "Terror of the Seventh Sea",' said Tom.

'I may have exaggerated,' the captain muttered.

The *Black Heart* was faster than the *Yohoho*. The ship quickly drew closer.

'Man the cannons!' yelled Captain Singh. 'They'll not take us without a fight!'

Tom and Daisy rushed to the nearest cannon. Tom loaded it. Daisy lit the fuse. They stood well back.

BANG!

Their shot fell just short. The cannonball hit the sea with a colossal splash.

Before they could fire again, the *Black Heart* was upon them.

With a roar, Captain Corkscrew leapt aboard the *Yohoho*. His pirate crew swarmed after him.

'Haa-harr!' bellowed the fearsome captain. 'Show 'em no mercy, lads!'

He rushed at Captain Singh's crew, swishing his metal hook.

'Here!' yelled Peg. 'Grab these!' She tossed Tom and Daisy a weapon each.

Tom, Daisy and the pirate crew fought bravely. The air rang with the sound of knife on fork. But Captain Corkscrew had too many men.

As Tom blocked another blow, a deck-hatch by his feet creaked open.

'Is all this noise *absolutely* necessary?' purred a familiar voice. 'I was trying to grab forty winks…'

'Jinx!' cried Daisy. 'So this is where you've been!'

To Tom and Daisy's surprise, Captain Corkscrew suddenly stopped fighting. He was staring in horror at Jinx.

'Ooooo! Arrgghh!' wailed Corkscrew. 'It's the Dread Pirate Claw! Get back to the ship, lads! Row for your lives!'

Shrieking and wailing, he and his terrified crew fled. They streamed overboard, back on to the *Black Heart*. Moments later, the ship was pulling away from the *Yohoho* at full speed.

Tom and Daisy watched the *Black Heart* sail into the distance. They were very relieved, and a little confused. Tom turned to Jinx.

'The "Dread Pirate Claw"?'

'What can I say?' purred Jinx. 'It seems I have a reputation.'

He winked his patchless eye.

The children wanted to hear more about Jinx's pirate career, but at that moment Poggins gave a yell.

'Land ahoy!'

# Chapter Six
# Yellowbeard's Treasure

The pirates had found Crossbone Island. Captain Singh was over the moon.

Tom and Daisy helped drop the *Yohoho*'s anchor and lower the ship's gig into the sea. The crew climbed aboard. They rowed towards a cove on the island shore. They dragged the gig up on to the beach.

Captain Singh checked his map.

'The X is here, look,' he said, pointing. 'And X marks the spot! Twenty paces north of the Hollow Tree. Come on – let's explore!'

They split up to search the island. It was Daisy who found the Hollow Tree. She did her very best, loudest wolf whistle. The others came running.

Poggins had brought the ship's compass – so they could find north. Tom stood with his back to the Hollow Tree. He took twenty paces in the right direction. His last stride brought him to the foot of another large tree.

'That's no good!' cried Tom. 'You can't bury treasure right under a great big tree! The map must be wrong!'

But Captain Singh was beaming from ear to ear.

'My precious Treasure!' cried the captain. 'At last!'

He wasn't looking at the ground beneath the tree. He was looking up into its branches. Perched on one of them was a beautiful bird. It swooped down from the tree and landed on Captain Singh's shoulder.

'Who's a pretty Polly?' it squawked. It began nibbling the captain's ear with its beak.

## Chapter Seven

# Pieces of Eight

'That's Treasure, the Captain's parrot,' Peg told Daisy. 'She went missing a few weeks ago. *That's* why he has been in such a grump.'

'And I would never have found her without your help!' the captain said. 'How can I thank you, me hearties?'

'A souvenir would be nice,' said Tom. 'To remember our pirate adventure by.'

'Pieces of eight!' squawked Treasure.

'That's a fine idea, my precious!' cried the captain. He pulled a handful of silver coins from his pocket. He gave one to Tom and one to Daisy.

'Wow! Real pieces of eight!' said Daisy. 'Look at these, Jinx!'

But Jinx wasn't there.

'He was by the Hollow Tree a moment ago,' said Peg.

The ancient tree's massive trunk really was totally hollow. It was pitch-black inside.

'I bet he went inside, for a sleep!' laughed Tom. 'I'll take a look!' He climbed into the dark hollow.

Minutes passed. Neither Tom nor Jinx reappeared. Daisy began to think they were teasing.

She climbed in after Tom...

…and stepped out on to Genie Street.

Tom was waiting for her, happily flipping his silver coin.

'We're back, then,' said Daisy.

'Yup!' said Tom. 'Pirate life was fun, wasn't it?'

'Though rather tiring,' purred Jinx, stretching. 'Now, you two had best get home or Captain Dad will shiver *your* timbers!'

The children took his advice, leaving the Dread Pirate Claw to have a well-earned nap.

7

GENIE STREET

# Mrs Proctor MONSTER DOCTOR

# Contents

## Chapter One
# A Creature in the Night

Daisy woke with a start. It was very dark in her room.

Something had just moved across her legs, she was sure. Something *alive*.

Daisy turned on her bedside lamp. With her eyes screwed up against the bright light, she peered at the foot of her bed.

'Jinx!'

The black and white cat was padding about impatiently on Daisy's duvet.

'At last!' he purred. 'I thought you'd *never* wake up!'

Daisy looked at her clock. It was just after midnight.

'But... why are you... how did...?' she mumbled sleepily.

'No time for questions!' purred Jinx. 'Up you get! You're needed in Lampland!'

Daisy didn't need telling twice. A trip to Lampland was unmissable – even in the middle of the night.

Tom's sleepy face appeared over the side of the top bunk. 'What's going on?'

Daisy explained. Her brother was up like a shot. He was just as keen to pay Lampland another visit.

They crept downstairs after Jinx. Silently, they slipped out of the front door, into the dark.

'First stop – the magic street lamp!' whispered Tom. The magic street lamp that stood outside the Genie Street shops always lit the way to Lampland. 'We need to give it the secret rub – *once up… once down… then three times round and round* – right, Jinx?'

'Wrong,' purred Jinx. 'I've seen to that myself. The lamp has already chosen you a door. Can't you tell?'

'I see it now!' said Daisy. 'Look, Tom – *there*!'

In the darkness, the door of one house on the opposite side of the street stood out clearly. It was glowing purple.

'Come on, then!' said Tom.

Suddenly, a headlight beam cut through the dark. The roar of an engine broke the silence. A motorcycle and sidecar came growling out of the night. It stopped beside the children.

## Chapter Two

# What's in the Box?

Tom and Daisy only recognized the motorcycle's rider when he took off his helmet and goggles.

'Mr Mistry!'

'Hullo, hullo!' beamed the Genie Street postman. 'Special Delivery for Mrs Proctor!' A large parcel was crammed into the sidecar. 'And it's *very* hefty, bless my ears!'

Tom and Daisy knew Mrs Proctor. She was the local vet. She lived opposite them, at number 10. It was *her* front door that was glowing.

They helped unload the heavy box, then struggled across the road with it.

'You weren't… kidding… Mr… Mistry!' grunted Tom, as they put the box down by the glowing door. 'It weighs a ton! What exactly is in here?'

There was no answer.

Mr Mistry, the motorcycle and the sidecar had all disappeared.

'It seems our friend couldn't hang around,' purred Jinx. 'Now, since you two are a little out of puff, allow me...'

He lifted a white-socked paw and knocked on Mrs Proctor's glowing front door.

The door vanished.

In its place was the entrance to a long, dark tunnel.

## Chapter Three
# The Monster Mountains

The tunnel was carved through solid rock. A cold draught came from its mouth. A tiny pinpoint of light marked its far end.

'After you!' purred Jinx.

Tom and Daisy struggled to lift the Special Delivery parcel again. They began making their way slowly along the murky passageway.

At last, they reached the tunnel's other end. It brought them out at the base of a high rock face – into broad daylight.

'I think my arms are coming off!' complained Daisy.

She and Tom put the parcel down on the rocky ground. They looked around. Tall grey mountains rose on all sides.

'We've not been to *this* part of Lampland before,' said Tom.

'Unless I'm much mistaken,' purred Jinx, 'we're in the Monster Mountains.'

Daisy shivered.

'Why *Monster* Mountains?' she said.

Before Jinx could reply, a blood-curdling howl filled the air.

A huge, hairy creature came stomping into view. It had thick green fur, a pair of enormous fangs and a single monstrous eye.

The creature gave another howl of rage. Without warning, it flung its massive body against the nearest wall of rock.

The ground shook. A shower of small rocks came clattering down the mountain's sloping sides.

'Watch out!' cried Tom as a tumbling boulder just missed him.

The monster heard. It turned and fixed Tom and Daisy with an angry, one-eyed stare.

# Chapter Four
# Knockout!

*Ffffff-ttt*!

Daisy heard something go whistling through the air. The monster let out a whimper. Its eye went wide with shock. Then its eyelid slowly drooped, and it staggered to one side.

Its huge body slumped to the floor with a mighty thud!

A woman stepped out from behind a nearby rock. She was carrying a peculiar weapon.

'Mrs Proctor!'

Tom and Daisy watched their Genie Street neighbour hurry over to the monster. She plucked a long silver dart from its leg.

'Don't worry – I haven't hurt him!' she told them. 'It's just a knockout dart, to put him to sleep for a bit.'

'I've been tracking him for a while,' Mrs Proctor went on. 'He's been taking his temper out on mountain after mountain. It's not like him. If he carries on like this, he'll set off an avalanche!'

She knelt down beside the monster's head. 'But I have a hunch why he's so grouchy. Let's take a look...'

She began examining the monster's huge mouth.

# Chapter Five
# Fang Rot

'Ah-ha!' cried Mrs Proctor. 'I knew it!' She was peering at one of the monster's awesome front teeth. 'It's a bad case of fang rot! I need to treat that immediately!'

'Is that what you do, then?' asked Daisy. 'Look after poorly monsters?'

'Exactly!' said Mrs Proctor.

'I've got *lots* of patients waiting back at my base camp surgery,' Mrs Proctor told the children. She looked at the sleeping monster. 'That's where this chap needs to be. I can't treat him here.' She frowned. 'But he's far too big and heavy to move.'

Then Tom had a brainwave. He looked at the Special Delivery parcel.

'I wonder...' he muttered.

'Fantastic!' cried Mrs Proctor.

Mr Mistry had delivered yet again. His parcel contained exactly what they needed.

It was an extra-large, extra-strong medical trolley – perfect for shifting a great, big heavy monster.

They quickly put the trolley together. With much huffing and puffing, they managed to get the monster on to it. Then they set off – with Jinx hitching a ride.

# Chapter Six
# Mrs Proctor's Surgery

With the trolley's help, it didn't take long to get the monster back to Mrs Proctor's surgery. It was a big white tent, pitched at the foot of the mountains.

Once inside the tent, Mrs Proctor wasted no time. She quickly chose a large pair of tooth-pulling pliers from her medical equipment.

Jinx went rather pale. 'I may just look away for a moment,' he purred.

Minutes later, Mrs Proctor proudly handed Tom a huge extracted monster fang.

'See – it's completely rotten in the middle!' she said. 'All that howling and temper was down to terrible toothache!'

The monster was already coming round. It got to its feet groggily. Tom and Daisy backed away.

But the monster didn't look angry any more. It grinned a wide, one-fanged grin. Then it put a massive furry arm round each of them, and gave them a friendly squeeze.

'What's your name?' said Tom. The monster looked puzzled.

'Why don't we call you... Fang?' suggested Daisy.

The monster grinned again.

Mrs Proctor had *lots* more patients waiting to see her.

The first was small, blue and covered in itchy spots.

'Monster pox!' said Mrs Proctor.

She asked Daisy to dab pink lotion all over the miserable monster's scaly skin.

Next came a three-headed monster with a headache. Tom helped give the poor creature the right dose of medicine – a bucketful for each head.

Both Daisy *and* Tom had to help with the next case. It took all three of them to pull a giant splinter out of the biggest big toe the children had ever seen.

'Excellent!' cried Mrs Proctor. 'I'm getting through patients *twice* as quickly with your help!'

Fang wanted to help, too. Mrs Proctor gave him a stethoscope to keep him quiet. He ate it.

Chapter Seven

# An Unlucky Shot

At last, all the monster patients had been treated. Mrs Proctor, Tom and Daisy were tired, but happy. Jinx was fast asleep on a box of monster nit combs.

Only Fang was still full of energy. He wanted to play. Daisy had to keep telling him not to touch things.

'Phew!' said Tom. 'That was pretty crazy! What about that ten-legged monster with athlete's foot? And the one wi–'

He was cut off by a shriek from Daisy.

'No, Fang! *NO*! Put that down before you hurt yourself!'

The big, green monster had got his paws on Mrs Proctor's dart gun. He was shaking it about, looking puzzled.

*Fffffff-ttt*! *Fffffff-ttt*!

Fang had accidentally set off both barrels of the dart gun.

Daisy felt a prick in her leg. She looked down. A silver knockout dart was sticking in her thigh.

'Ow!' yelped Tom. The second dart had hit him in the arm. 'What… wassssss…?' His voice slurred.

Daisy's eyes began to fog over. She felt herself falling. Then everything went black.

# Chapter Eight
# Back to Bed

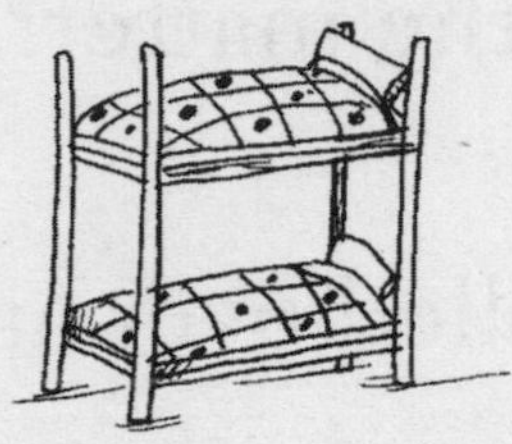

Daisy came round slowly. She was back in bed, in her room.

'*Ooooo*! W-w-what... happened?' Tom's groggy voice came from the bunk above. 'One moment we're in the Monster Mountains and the next...'

Daisy smiled to herself. It hadn't been a dream, then.

Tom gave a sudden yelp.

'What's the matter?' said Daisy.

'I just rolled over and something poked me!' said Tom. A moment later, his grinning face appeared. He was holding Fang's extracted tooth.

'How's *that* for a souvenir?'

Daisy grinned back.

'Just like our monster adventure,' she replied. '*Fang-tastic*!'

Here's what other children have to say about Genie Street and their favourite Lampland characters!

'My favourite story was *Doctor Singh, Pirate King* because it was really exciting. It made me want to go to Lampland and be on a pirate ship, too.' Aaron, age 6

'I really liked the books about Lampland – can we have more of them in our classroom, please?' Miriam, age 6

'When they rubbed the lamp I was so excited but also a little bit scared about what would happen. This book is fantastic and I hope I can read more like it.' Shantai, age 5

'I liked all the monsters because they weren't really angry monsters at all, they were just poorly.' Jenaih, age 6

'It was an exciting adventure story. I feel like I want to read more and more, and I would also like to visit Lampland. It is a really exciting place.' Abdul, age 6

# Parent note

Genie Street is a brand-new fiction series that is the next step up from Ladybird's Read it yourself Level 4. Ideal for newly independent Key Stage 1 readers, these books are for children who want to read real fiction for the first time.

## Collect all the titles in the series:

9781409312390

9781409312406

9781409312413

9781409312420

9781409312437

9781409312444

Each book contains two easy-to-read stories that children will love. The stories include short chapters, simple vocabulary and a clear layout that will encourage and build confidence when reading.